MUTANT WEREWOLF

by Richard Taylor
Illustrated by Mark Penman

Titles in Ignite

Badger Publishing Limited
Suite G08, Stevenage,
Hertfordshire SG1 2DX
Telephone: 01438 791037   Fax: 01438 791036
www.badgerlearning.co.uk

Mutant Baby Werewolf ISBN 978-1-84926-957-5

Publisher: Susan Ross
Senior Editor: Danny Pearson
Designer: Fiona Grant
Illustrator: Mark Penman

MUTANT BABY WEREWOLF

Contents

Vocabulary:

business   villains
babysitting   howling
cowering   burglars

Main characters:

Sophie

Lucy

Mr and Mrs George

Henry

Chapter 1
Easy money

Lucy and Sophie needed cash.

They needed to find a job. So they started up a business.

It was a babysitting business. "Babysitting is easy money," said Sophie. "You just watch TV while the kids sleep."

They put up an advert in their street.

The next day they found a job. Looking after Henry George.

Henry was the little boy next door to Lucy. A cute one-year-old. But Lucy's mum warned the girls about Mr and Mrs George.

"They're very fussy about their house," she said. "Don't make a mess and don't break anything!"

Lucy and Sophie knocked on Mr and Mrs George's house at eight. Sophie had brought a DVD with her. A horror called 'The Wolf Man'.

"Hello," said Mr George, who was a hairy-looking guy. "Little Henry is fast asleep. You'll have an easy job."

"We have a few rules," warned Mrs George. "Help yourself to food, but don't touch my cake. I've made it for a competition."

"And don't go near my model planes!" said Mr George, "Or my prize marrows."

Lucy looked at Sophie. Mum had been right.

"And be nice to Pongo," said Mrs George.

Pongo was her moody little cat. "She'll miss her mummy awfully…"

"Where are you off to?" asked Lucy.

Mr George grinned. "The Full Moon Ball," he said. "My wife and I go every few weeks, when the moon is full."

Mrs George giggled.

"And we'd better be off," Mr George said. "Any problems, just call!"

What problems could there be?
Easy money, thought the girls.

The Georges drove off under the bright full moon.

"Let's get that DVD on," said Sophie.

Chapter 2
Henry's secret

The movie was pretty scary. The Wolf Man was chasing some girl in the woods.

"Stop it a minute," said Lucy. "I want to get some crisps."

Sophie stopped the film.

Lucy went into the kitchen. Suddenly, she heard a scary, howling noise.

"Sophie! I asked you to stop the movie," said Lucy.

"I did," said Sophie. "It came from there."

She pointed at the baby-monitor!

"Henry!" gasped the girls.

They ran up to his room, but Henry was gone. The curtains had been ripped and the window was broken. The girls were frightened.

Then they heard the howling noise coming from the garden.

They ran down the stairs and out through the door.

There, in the middle of Mr George's prize marrows, sat a fuzzy little beast.

"Is that a puppy?" asked Sophie.

"No. It's a wolf cub," said Lucy. "I've seen them on TV."

The cub was munching through the marrows.

"Do you think it… ate Henry?" asked Sophie.

"No," said Lucy, thinking of their movie. "I think… I think… it IS Henry!"

It was true. The wolf pup looked just like him.

Wolf Henry stood up. He smiled cheekily at the girls.

"Do you think he's a..."

Suddenly, Pongo the cat sprang from the bush. Lucy and Sophie jumped.

Pongo ran into the house with Henry chasing him.

"After them!" shouted Lucy.

Chapter 3

Henry on the loose

Henry chased Pongo all the way up to the loft. The loft where Mr George kept his model planes.

When the girls got there, they saw a bright purple cat hissing in the corner. Henry had knocked a can of model paint all over Pongo.

"We're in big trouble," said Sophie.

Henry now had one of Mr George's planes in his mouth.

"No, Henry! Naughty wolf-pup!" shouted Sophie.

Henry just giggled.

Suddenly, the doorbell rang. The girls darted downstairs.

It was Lucy's mum. "What's all the noise?" she asked.

"We were just watching a movie with the sound turned up," said Sophie.

"OK," said Mum. "I was a bit worried."

Mum left. The girls had fooled her.
But what had Henry done while they'd
been away?

Lucy heard a noise from the kitchen.
It sounded like snoring.

Henry was fast asleep in Mrs George's
special cake. He was covered in crumbs.
How would they explain this one?

Suddenly, the light faded. The moon
had been covered by cloud. Before
their eyes, Henry turned back into a
little human.

Lucy picked the sleeping boy up and took him back to his cot.

"We'd better tidy up," said Sophie. "Mr and Mrs George are going to go mad!"

"And how will we tell them that their son's a werewolf?"

Lucy and Sophie started in the loft, trying to fix Mr George's models.
It looked like the end of their babysitting business.

Lucy could hear talking downstairs.

The Georges must be back, she thought.

"Let's tell them we did it. Better than telling them their son's a mutant."

The girls bounded down the stairs. They felt sick with nerves.

But when they entered the living room it was not the Georges they met.

It was two rough-looking men. Two men filling up bags.

Chapter 4

Skinner and Tony

Before they could run, the burglars grabbed Lucy and Sophie.

"Who are you two?" asked the bigger man.

"Babysitters," said Sophie.

"I thought you said the house was empty, Skinner? Watch them while I clean it out."

"OK, Tony," said Skinner. He shoved the girls onto the sofa.

"Shut up and don't move," he said. Tony headed up the stairs.

Tears filled the scared girls' eyes. Tony was going to find Henry.

At that moment, Lucy spotted the full moon coming out from the clouds.

The first thing they heard was that scary howling noise coming from the monitor.

"What the…?"

Then they heard a growl. Then a bark. Then a scream.

Skinner looked scared. "You got a dog up there?"

"Kind of…" said Sophie. The girls smiled.

Another growl came from the monitor, followed by a scream of pain.

"Tony!" Skinner cried. He darted out of the door and up the stairs to save his friend.

When the girls entered Henry's bedroom, they found the little wolf-cub with his teeth clamped on Skinner's leg. Skinner was trying to shake him off. Tony was cowering in the corner, his clothes torn to shreds.

"Call that thing off. Please!" He sobbed.

Henry started to tear Skinner's shirt.

"Henry – cuddle!" shouted Lucy.

Henry stopped. He turned to Lucy, smiled and jumped into her arms.

The burglars saw their chance. They ran for their lives.

"Good Henry!" said Sophie, rubbing the little wolf's tummy.

Chapter 5
The Georges return

As Lucy and Sophie patted the brave little werewolf, cloud covered up the moon again.

The fierce little cub turned back into a gurgling baby.

Outside, a siren wailed. A few minutes later, the police arrived at the house with Lucy's mum.

"What happened?" asked Mum.
"I heard men screaming, so I called the police. I was scared."

"We managed to catch them," said the policeman. "They're locked up in the van."

"But what did you do to them?" asked the other policeman. "Those tough guys were crying like children. They kept talking about a monster?"

Lucy looked at Sophie. Henry giggled.

"We heard them upstairs, so we turned the horror movie up to full blast," said Sophie. "It must have scared them."

"Good thinking," said Lucy's mum.

"They jumped over the fence. Mr Johnson's dog must have got them," said Lucy.

"Amazing," laughed the policeman.

At that point, Mr and Mrs George came home. Mrs George grabbed her little son. "My baby!" she said.

The police told Mr and Mrs George the story. Lucy and Sophie told them how the burglars crushed Mrs George's cake and broke Mr George's planes. They even smashed his marrows.

"Animals!" said Mr George.

"But worst of all…" said Lucy, "they threw purple paint all over Pongo!"

Mrs George gasped. Henry chuckled.

"Well," said Mrs George, "the main thing is that everyone is OK."

"And," said the policeman, "there's a big reward for catching those two villains."

The next day, Lucy and Sophie gave up babysitting. It was not as easy as they had thought. The Georges would have to stay at home for the next Full Moon Dance.

They may get a surprise, thought Lucy.

Sophie spent her reward money on a load of new horror movies.

Lucy was thinking about buying a puppy.

But they both agreed to buy Henry a box of new toys.

And maybe a few dog biscuits.

Facts about wolves

The grey wolf is the largest member of the dog family.

Wolves were once found all over the world.

Can you believe there were once many wolves in Britain? But sadly, because they have been hunted and their homes have been destroyed by humans, they are now only found in a few places, such as North America and Sweden.

Wolves are like human beings because they live in families and even have a partner – a bit like a husband and wife.

Wolves can communicate over a long distance by howling.

They hunt other animals, such as sheep, but the only animal that a wolf fears is a human being!

Wolves are often found in stories and myths. There are a lot in the folk-tales of Native Americans.

Many stories and myths speak of humans changing into wolf-like creatures, but we all know this cannot be true... can it?

Questions

What was the name of the DVD Sophie had with her?

Where were Mr and Mrs George going?

What pet is the wolf related to?

How do wolves communicate?

What is a 'predator'? Is a wolf a 'predator'?

Can you find out which countries wolves live in?

What is a myth?